For Nicholas, Natalie, and Hannah,
and for my own Tooth Fairies
—Brooke

To Anita, Lauri, and Lisa
—Deborah

Sleeping Bear Press thanks reporter Noah Bacheller (aka Noah Fang)
for his incisive reporting for the *The Tooth Fairy Times*.

Text Copyright © 2020 Brooke Hecker
Illustration Copyright © 2020 Deborah Melmon
Design © 2020 Sleeping Bear Press

SLEEPING BEAR PRESS™

2395 South Huron Parkway, Suite 200
Ann Arbor, MI 48104
www.sleepingbearpress.com
© Sleeping Bear Press

Printed and bound in the United States.
10 9 8 7 6 5 4 3 2 1

Library of Congress Cataloging-in-Publication Data
Names: Hecker, Brooke, author. | Melmon, Deborah, illustrator.
Title: Letters from my Tooth Fairy / written by Brooke Hecker ; illustrated by Deborah Melmon.
Description: Ann Arbor, MI : Sleeping Bear Press, [2020] | Audience: Ages 4-8.
Summary: "Over the course of five years, a little girl and her tooth fairy
exchange letters, asking and answering questions about some
of childhood's most important moments, including bad school
pictures and best-friend troubles"– Provided by publisher.
Identifiers: LCCN 2020006243 | ISBN 9781534110557 (hardcover)
Subjects: CYAC: Tooth Fairy–Fiction. | Teeth–Fiction. | Letters–Fiction.
Classification: LCC PZ7.1.H43534 Let 2020 | DDC [E]–dc23
LC record available at https://lccn.loc.gov/2020006243

Letters from My Tooth Fairy

written by Brooke Hecker

Illustrated by Deborah Melmon

Natalie

Published by Sleeping Bear Press™

Tooth 1: The Very First Tooth
(Bottom Central Incisor 1)

Dear Natalie,

I am so excited to meet you! (Well, almost. You were fast asleep and snoring when I stopped by.) I am your Tooth Fairy, and I was assigned to your teeth as soon as your first baby tooth erupted, which in your case was when you were five months old. I have been waiting over six years to come back—that's a really long time when you love teeth as much as I do!

Thank you so much for leaving me this exquisite incisor. It is as gleaming and clean as I imagined. (Great job with the toothbrushing.) Keep putting your lost teeth under your pillow, and each time I will leave you a little bit of money in return. I can't wait to collect the other nineteen in the set!

Love, *Your Tooth Fairy*

Dear Tooth Fairy,
Thank you for the money last time. I put it in my piggy bank. My parents said there will be a blizzard. Will you still be able to get here?

Sincerely, Natalie

Dear Natalie,

The weatherman was right—it's a mess out there. You know how much I love teeth—teeth are my life!—but when my Tooth Fairy alarm rang tonight, all I wanted to do was stay inside with my warmest blanket and a hot cup of cocoa. Duty calls, though, and no matter how bad the storm, Tooth Fairies prevail.

Stay warm, *Your Tooth Fairy*

Dear Natalie,

You are famous! This afternoon, I opened the *Tooth Fairy Times* and there you were on the front page. It was the lead article accompanied by a huge photo of you. Sweetheart, you did NOT look happy. I wouldn't be happy either if I had been playing tag at recess and the WALL hit my FACE. The good news (for me!) is that the wall popped out your top incisor, right there in front of the entire second grade (and two third graders who were walking to the bathroom behind the basketball hoop).

Judging by your swollen lips, that must have been both very painful and mortifying. I was proud to read that you stood tall and brave the entire rest of the day. I tell ya, kid, I knew you were special.

With pride and love,

Your Tooth Fairy

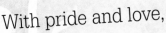

THE Tooth Fairy TIMES

Hitting a WALL
Local girl loses tooth during recess

BY NOAH W. FANG

Interviews from eye witnesses on page 2

Interviews from eye witnesses on page 2

It was a chilly, rainy day at Quarton Elementary School and, due to the inclement weather, the children went to the gym for recess.

Natalie, a second grader in Ms. Wind's class, was playing tag in the gym when she was tagged IT by a friend. Instantly, she started racing after the closest student. Natalie almost tagged the student, but they took a quick turn, and Natalie went face first into the wall popping out her top central incisor.

There have been two other similar tooth-loss incidents in Quarton Elementary's 93-year history. The first, in 1975, occurred when an intense game of dodgeball resulted in a missing top lateral incisor.

(See RECESS, page 2)

UPDATE FROM CITY COUNCIL MEETING

The Tooth Fairy City Council meeting was held last Tuesday, and the main topic of discussion was Big Tooth Fairy Dust Factory raising the price of fairy dust. Fairies want more money for the teeth they collect in order to pay the children, as well as cover the cost of purchasing fairy dust from the factory.

"We are willing to lower the cost of our new and current lines of fairy dust," said Ben Molarloch, president of Big Tooth Fairy Dust. Vice president Heather Flossington also commented that the company will look into paying more for teeth with little to no tarter. Removing tarter before grinding teeth can be expensive for the factory, so eliminating the additional cost of tarter removal will result in a savings for the factory, which will be passed on to the Tooth Fairies. The local association of Tooth Fairies will work with dentists to get the word out on better brushing habits to children all over the area.

Photo credit: Principal Dooley

Tooth Fairy Society Annual Award Show Results Page 6

TOOTH FAIRY DUST COMPANY ANNOUNCES NEW COLORS!

The Tooth Fairy Dust Company has announced its new color for the year. The color was revealed at the latest Tooth Fairy Conference in California. Thousands of Tooth Fairies attended the conference and were thrilled to learn the new color is Ocean Blue. With ToothTone naming "classic blue" its color of the year, Tooth Fairy Dust Company has followed suit.

This color has versatile appeal with all Tooth Fairies around the country. It infuses "tradition with confidence," said Dust Fairy head designer, dusty Sprinkles. Mr. Sprinkles went on to say the most popular...

Fairies...
you...
I w...
Mia...
lot...
I wo...
not...
brie...

Fair...
exc...
ment...
color...
yello...
fairy...
will r...
Fairies...
to add more choices to their collection.

Natalie tonight

Weather:
Low of 32 degrees!
Frost delays in the interior region

Dear Natalie,

Yay! It's your second lost top incisor. You probably hate it, but there is nothing cuter than the oh-so-fleeting gap-toothed smile of a kid who loses both of their front top teeth. It's like a rainbow—it doesn't last long, but it is soooo cool while it's there. AND JUST IN TIME FOR SCHOOL PICTURES. Do me a favor, will you? Leave me a photo with your next tooth.

Love,

Your Tooth Fairy

Dear Tooth Fairy,

Why are my new teeth so big? Are they going to grow even bigger? Please say no! I look like a walrus.

Sincerely,

Natalie

P.S. Here is my school picture.

Dear Natalie,

Excellent question! Your permanent teeth erupt in full size. Right now, your mouth is still small, so the new teeth feel too big. Don't worry—your mouth will grow but the teeth won't. You'll look less walrus-like in no time.

Hang in there, Your Tooth Fairy

P.S. Love the picture!

Dear Natalie,

You should have given me a heads-up on the new bunk bed! I know that I can fly and all, but I am a little scared of heights. When you are five inches tall, the top of a bunk bed may as well be the top of the Empire State Building. I am proud to say that I pulled myself together for your latest incisor, because I knew that you were depending on me, and being dependable is crucial for a Tooth Fairy.

Oh, and Natalie? Next time you lose a tooth, please sleep on the bottom bunk. ☺

Love, *Your Tooth Fairy*

Dear Natalie,

Picture this: I'm flying in to grab your latest incisor, and I crash right into a crib that wasn't there before. Inside that never-there-before crib was a new BABY. I've been to your room six times now, and surely I would have noticed a crib AND a baby. By the way, the baby was definitely NOT sleeping, and I swear she looked right at me. Rule #1 in Tooth Fairy law is to NEVER, not EVER, be spotted by children. Thank my lucky stars that babies cannot talk!

Congratulations on being a big sister! Sure, baby sisters can be annoying, but you now have a friend for life. The baby is probably getting a lot of gifts, so here is a little something extra just for you.

Love,

Your Tooth Fairy

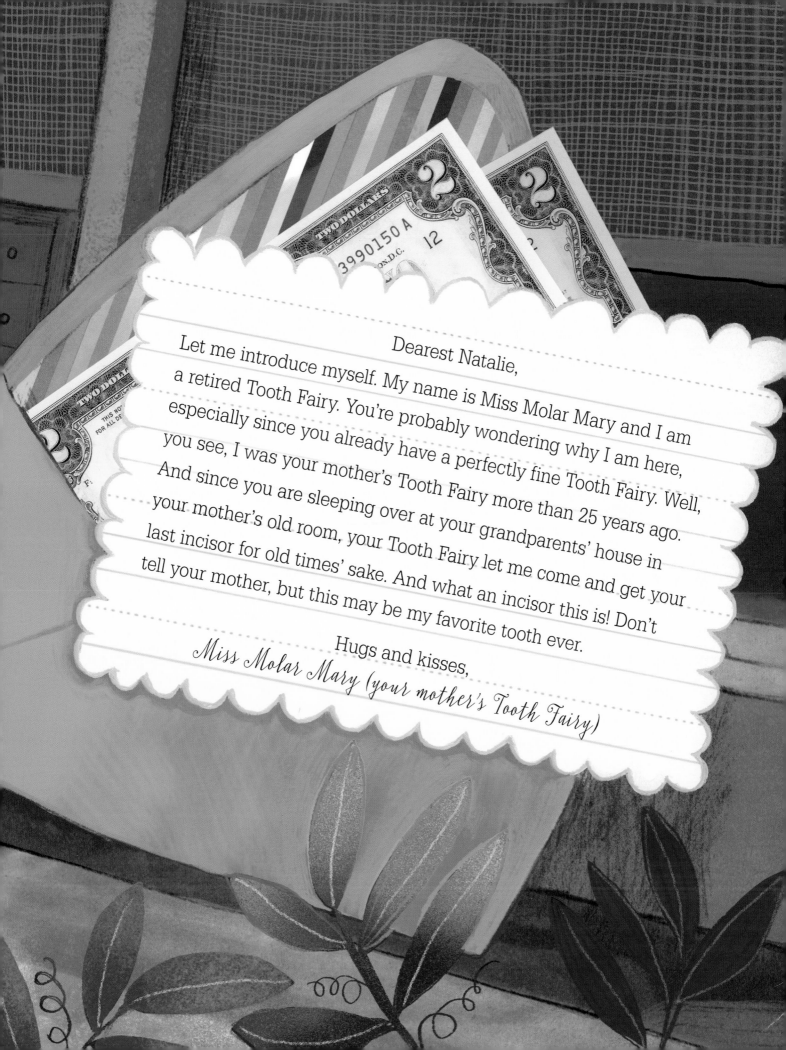

Dearest Natalie,

Let me introduce myself. My name is Miss Molar Mary and I am a retired Tooth Fairy. You're probably wondering why I am here, especially since you already have a perfectly fine Tooth Fairy. Well, you see, I was your mother's Tooth Fairy more than 25 years ago. And since you are sleeping over at your grandparents' house in your mother's old room, your Tooth Fairy let me come and get your last incisor for old times' sake. And what an incisor this is! Don't tell your mother, but this may be my favorite tooth ever.

Hugs and kisses,
Miss Molar Mary (your mother's Tooth Fairy)

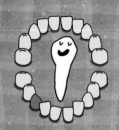

Dear Natalie,

You won't BELIEVE what happened last night. I was flying through your window like always and I turned off my fairy flashlight, because I know that your little sister wakes easily. It was dark, but I thought, No problem. I'm a professional; I can handle the dark. Then, just as I got to your bed and swooped down toward your pillow, my foot got caught in your fabulous NEW solar system mobile. Now, I am all for space exploration but I was just dangling there. Not a pretty picture. I panicked and thrashed about until— PLOP! I landed right ON YOUR HEAD, NATALIE!

And you know what happened? Nothing. You slept right through it. Sorry for leaving a little fairy dust in your hair, but I think it looks really pretty.

Sweet dreams, *Your Tooth Fairy*

Tooth 10: Moving
(Bottom Cuspid 2)

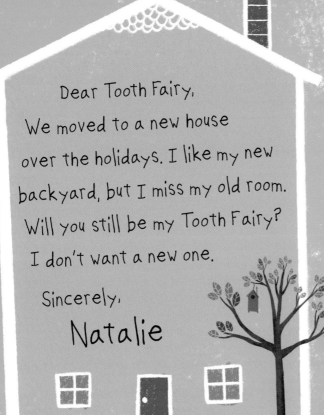

Dear Tooth Fairy,

We moved to a new house over the holidays. I like my new backyard, but I miss my old room. Will you still be my Tooth Fairy? I don't want a new one.

Sincerely,

Natalie

Dear Natalie,

Of course! I am still your Tooth Fairy, no matter where you live. I know that moving is hard, but look how much more space you have. I love your new room, by the way. Is that Bubble-Gum Pink on the walls? Great choice.

Along with the usual money, I am leaving you this shimmery fairy night-light for your beautiful new room (that you don't have to share anymore!).

Still yours, *Your Tooth Fairy*

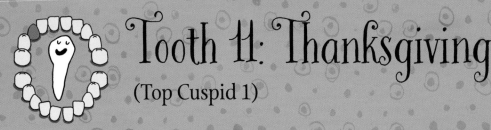

Dear Natalie,

In all my years as a Tooth Fairy, this is my very first Thanksgiving tooth. You would think that this would happen a lot on a holiday like Thanksgiving, with all the eating. It turns out, though, that most Thanksgiving dishes are quite mushy: Grandma's fluffy mashed potatoes, Aunt Birdie's yam soufflé, and, best of all, the silkiest, creamiest pumpkin pie made this year by . . . YOU. I wish you would have saved me a piece!

Happy Thanksgiving,

Your Tooth Fairy

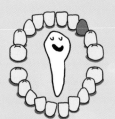

Dear Tooth Fairy,

Guess what? My tooth fell out while I was sleeping. I was afraid that I swallowed it, but then my dad found it by the side of my bed. What would happen if I had swallowed it?

Yours truly,
Natalie

Dear Natalie,

This happens way more often than you think. In fact, it is probably one of the most popular questions that I get (other than "What do you do with the teeth?"—which is TOP SECRET). In most cases, if a kid swallows a tooth, it will come out the next day when they go to the bathroom.

I'm sure glad that it didn't, though—because once that cuspid's flushed, I'm not going after it!

Love,

Your Tooth Fairy

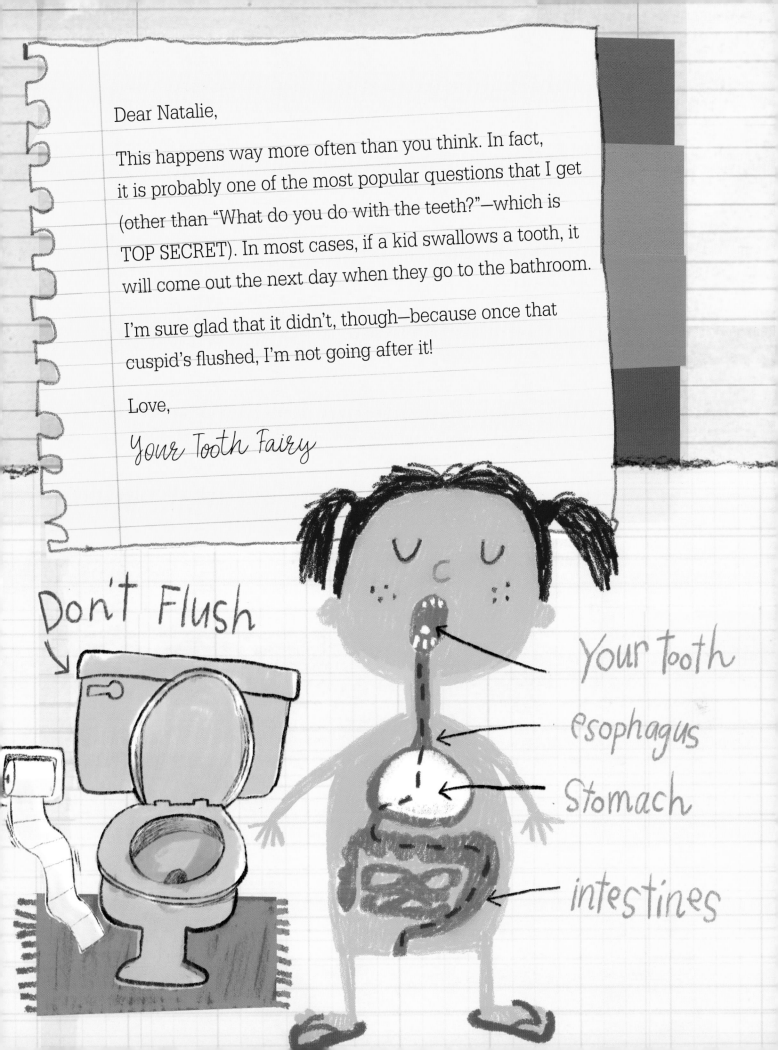

Don't Flush

Your tooth

esophagus

Stomach

intestines

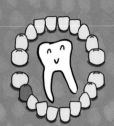

Dear Tooth Fairy,

My mom pulled my tooth out and it hurt so bad, and blood even got on my favorite shirt. Can you please tell her not to do that ever again?

Yours Truly,

Natalie

Dear Natalie,

I did a little investigating into the Mom tooth-pulling situation. What seems to have happened is that your primary molar was hanging by a thread, and she became concerned that it might come out in your sleep again. There was also a rumor that you and your cousin were planning to tie a string to the tooth, tie the other end of the string to the door, and SLAM THE DOOR. I've seen that kind of maneuver go badly, so I understand why your mom intervened. I assure you that she has learned her lesson.

Love, Your Tooth Fairy

Dear Tooth Fairy,

I have a problem. I lost my tooth in the school cafeteria, and I put it in the small section of my backpack, where I keep my pencils and stuff. When I got home, it was gone! I swear I checked everywhere! What happens now?

XOXO,
Natalie

P.S. Does this mean I don't get any money??

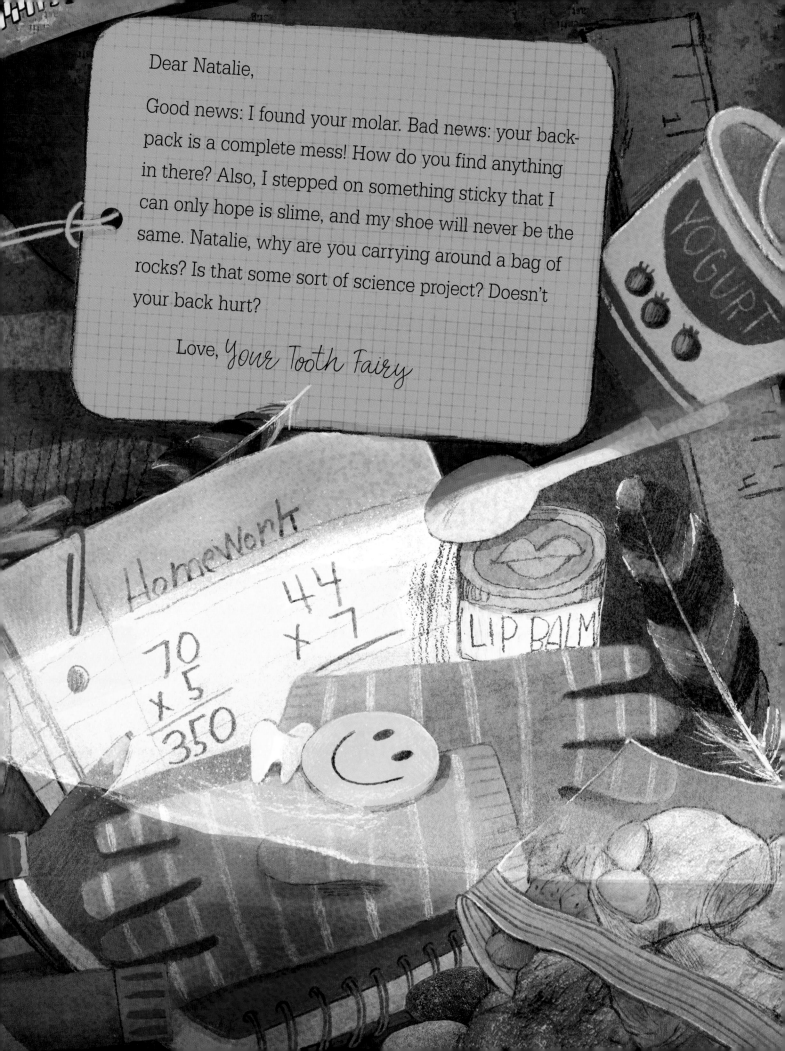

Dear Natalie,

Good news: I found your molar. Bad news: your back-pack is a complete mess! How do you find anything in there? Also, I stepped on something sticky that I can only hope is slime, and my shoe will never be the same. Natalie, why are you carrying around a bag of rocks? Is that some sort of science project? Doesn't your back hurt?

Love, *Your Tooth Fairy*

Dear Miss. T.,

I really hate to ask, but this time can you please leave a little more money? There is this game that I REALLY want and Chloe on my bus gets $10 per tooth, so maybe I can get $10, too?

XOXO, Natalie

Dear Natalie,

I am proud of you for asking so politely, but it is my policy to give a certain amount of money per tooth. True, some other Tooth Fairies give more, but there are also a lot of Tooth Fairies who give less, and I think that you get a perfectly fair amount. Maybe you can ask your parents if there is anything that you can do around the house to earn extra money? I couldn't help but notice that your lawn could use some raking ... Just an idea!

Good luck,

Your Tooth Fairy

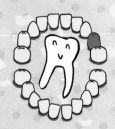
Dear Natalie,

I was on my way to a New Year's Eve party when I got the call. The Annual Fairy Ball Drop was at midnight, which should have been fine since you typically are asleep by 9:00 p.m. and it only takes me about half an hour to make the trip to your house. Easy peasy. Except NOT EASY PEASY, Natalie, because you decided to stay up until midnight! I waited by your window until 11:00 p.m., just hoping that you would nod off, but NO, you were perfectly awake. Finally I decided to go back to my party, see the ball drop, and then fly BACK to your house (at nearly 1:30 a.m.!) to retrieve your molar. I am exhausted.

Happy New Year, *Your Tooth Fairy*

P.S. They say that a tooth lost on New Year's Eve brings a whole year of good luck.

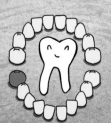

Tooth 17: Camp Timberwood
(Bottom Second Primary Molar A)

Heya, Natalie,

It's the Camp Timberwood Tooth Fairy here, coming to your bunk with the heartiest Timba-Timba-WOOOO. Your molar is my first tooth of the summer. Camp's great, isn't it? Swimming, tennis, music club—and did I hear you water-skied last week? Way to go, Natster!

In keeping with Camp Timberwood tradition, instead of money, I've made you this friendship bracelet. All green for color war (Go Bunk 5!).

Smell ya later,

The Timberwood Tooth Fairy

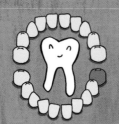

Dear Miss T.,

I lost another tooth today, but I am not even that excited because school was kind of bad and my friend Emily was mad at me all day for something I didn't even do.

I also worked really hard on my audition for the school play just to get a lame part with only three lines. Plus, losing a tooth just reminds me that my mom and dad said I need to get braces soon. Ugh.

XoXo,
Natalie

Dear Natalie,

I'm sorry that you had a bad day. Being a kid can be hard sometimes, especially in the sixth grade. I promise there will be many more good times than bad. We don't always get the parts we want, when we want them, but if you work hard and keep trying, you will get there eventually. As for the braces, I won't lie to you—braces are annoying. It will be worth it, though, when you get that million-dollar smile at the end.

Hang in there, *Your Tooth Fairy*

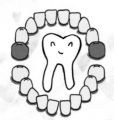

19 and 20: Braces
(Top Second Primary Molars A and B)

Dear Natalie,

Today must have been tough. Lots of kids go through it—your last molars were pulled to get ready for braces. The shot probably hurt for a minute, but then you didn't feel a thing when the dentist pulled your teeth, right? Knowing you, you were probably very brave. You know the best medicine to help you recover? Ice cream! Tell your mom I said so. I'm an expert.

Well, Natalie, these two molars are the last of your baby teeth. I can't believe the amazing twelve-year-old in front of me is the same little girl who I first met six years ago. It's always sad for me to say goodbye, but I am so proud to have watched you grow up. Thank you for twenty of the loveliest teeth in my collection.

Love always,

Your Tooth Fairy

P.S. I might be back to your house soon. I hear that your sister has her first loose incisor!